Daniel McCartney was a hard-working dedicated Deputy Sheriff and former city of Hoquaim Police Department Officer. Daniel loved his job and worked closely with his partners and friends in the Mountain Detachment in South Pierce County Washington. Daniel loved his family and was active in his church, his gym and community. Daniel always helped out anyone that needed it. Daniel McCartney was the best example of an honest person, a loving father, a committed husband and an amazing police Officer. Daniel inspired many of us and we honor his life by living ours as he did. His story lives on. This book is dedicated to his memory.

-Deputy Luke Baker
Partner of Daniel McCartney
K9 Handler of Dan

Daniel McCartney died in the Line Of Duty January 8th, 2018
chasing armed subjects who had just committed a home invasion Robbery

K-9 DAN

BY **MADISON MEADOWS**

ILLUSTRATED BY **NADYA SKY**

GRAY STREET
PUBLISHING

K-9 Dan

Copyright ©2019 by Madison Meadows

Illustrations by Nadya Sky

ISBN-13: 978-1-970083-03-3
ISBN-10: 1-970083-03-4

Hi, my name is K-9 Dan. It is nice to meet you! Thank you for being here with me today to tell my story. When I was born, I knew that I wanted to grow up and be a dog that helped make the world a safer place to live.

I was born in Hungary which is in Central Europe surrounded by Slovenia, Austria, Slovakia, Croatia, Romania, and Serbia. I had no idea that I would get on an airplane and travel all the way across the world to fulfill my mission.

After my airplane ride, I went to Shallow Creek Kennels in Pennsylvania to be trained. They said I am good at tracking, able to follow a scent, and was not distracted from what I am supposed to search. I was a good candidate to work for the police.

They taught me to be confident and courageous. I knew I still had to build my skills. After leaving Pennsylvania, I moved to Washington State and started the real work. I met a family that recently lost their father in the line of duty. He was a very courageous man. His name is Deputy Daniel McCartney. They decided to name me Dan after him. I had a lot to live up to.

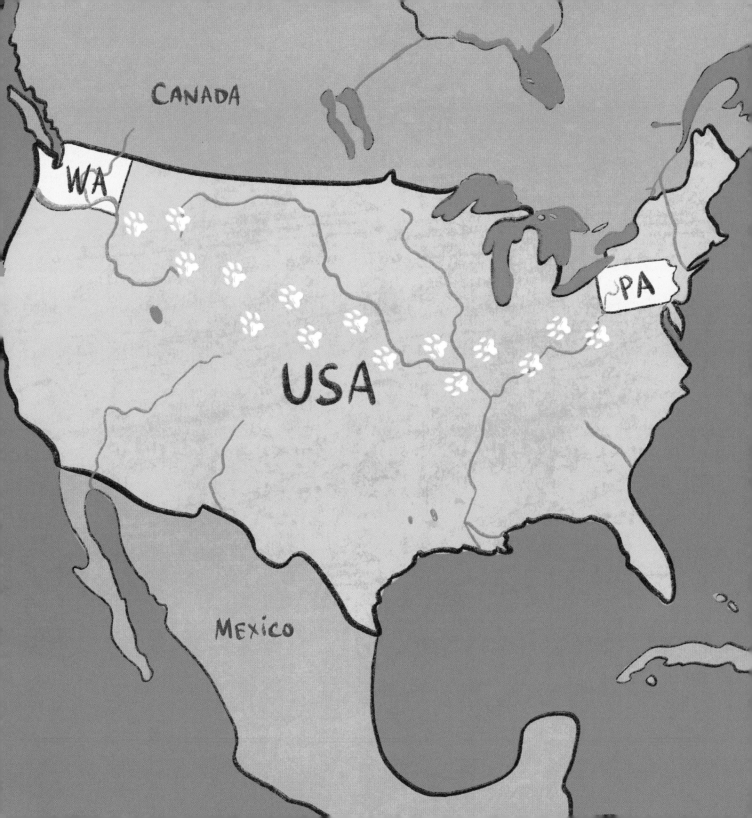

After I received my name, I started working on the 400 more hours of training and testing to be certified by the state to work alongside my partner, He is a human Deputy that has been trained to handle a dog with my skills and that is when I received my own BADGE!

My training was intense. I did agility courses (those were so much fun); I had to learn how to control myself and listen to directions. I also learned about the dangers and differences of working inside and tracking outside. Following a trail is serious business. My training doesn't stop; I always need to be trained more and reminded of my skills to be the best I can be.

Sometimes, I even get to wear a bulletproof vest. It was finally time for my first real job. A neighboring police agency called and needed me. I knew I could do this. I tracked and found the suspect in a creek who was wanted by the police.

Since my first job being K-9 Deputy Dan I have found many more people, some hiding in boats, cars, under houses, in trees and bushes. I have also helped find firearms and other evidence dropped by fleeing suspects. One of my other skills is helping to locate lost people.

We are part of a County-City Metro canine team and work a large area. We assist many communities.

Sometimes I am in the city tracking someone, running between buildings and around people; other times I am in the woods. These are the reasons I have so much training. I need to stay on track with whatever scent I am following. There are various smells in the city. I can't be distracted by a smell from a restaurant. When I have located and captured my suspect, I get lots of praise and treats.

I love my job and the rewards of fun during my time off. I love to play frisbee, tug of war, and race. They are all my favorites. I also know I need to rest to be on top of my skills. I love my human Deputy, my nice house and yard that give me a place to play, rest, eat, and sleep. I work hard, but that is why I can make a difference.

I trust my human Deputy, and he trusts me since we have had so much training together. We have even gone to schools and community events. This is where I have to be on my best behavior, even if I see a cat, I must not get distracted. Meeting people is fun.

When I am in my patrol vehicle and the door opens, I know if my human Deputy needs help or we are just getting out by how he acts and what he says to me. I also know I won't get lost because of special tracking done by a support helicopter.

My life is everything I dreamed it would be when I was a puppy. Everybody should choose to help someone when they can and be the best that they can be, always.

ABOUT THE AUTHOR

Madison Meadows lives in the Pacific Northwest and is a parent to three children and grandmother to two granddaughters. Besides writing, she spends some time creating cards and holds ownership in Gray Street Publishing out of Seattle.

K-9 Dan is the fourth children's book written by Madison Meadows. Her other titles are *Busy in Boots*, *Introducing Beebo*, and *Beebo's Ocean Vacation*, the second in the Beebo series. With this series and other books, she hopes to encourage and inspire all children to become better contributors to society.

Made in the USA
Monee, IL
31 March 2021